FOR THE LOVE OF A LADY BUG

By Imogene Forte
and Joy Mac Kenzie

Illustrated by GAYLE S. HARVEY

A KID'S STUFF BOOK

Printed in the United States of America

Library of Congress catalog card number: 77-83783
ISBN number: 0-913916-89-7

For Kristen, Shana and Jennifer

LADYBUG MINE . . .

What does a ladybug do all day?
Just flit through the grasses
And eat and play?
Where does she come from?
Just where does she go?
Is she really a lady?
How can you know
If she sleeps — or takes baths?
How does she talk?
How far on those tiny six legs
Can she walk?
Ladybug, Ladybug, whisper to me
Tell me your secrets — I'll keep them —
You'll see!

Use playdough and toothpicks
to make your very own
ladybug — just like me!
Remember, all insects have
three main body parts and
six legs.
Don't forget to give me a
name!

MENU FOR AN OUT-OF-DOORS FEAST

Make a lovely out-of-doors feast for your dolls, toys and animal
friends — and don't forget to invite a ladybug!
Use shells and leaves and stones for cups and dishes.
Use a puddle for a sink, flat rocks for a stove and sticks
for stirring.

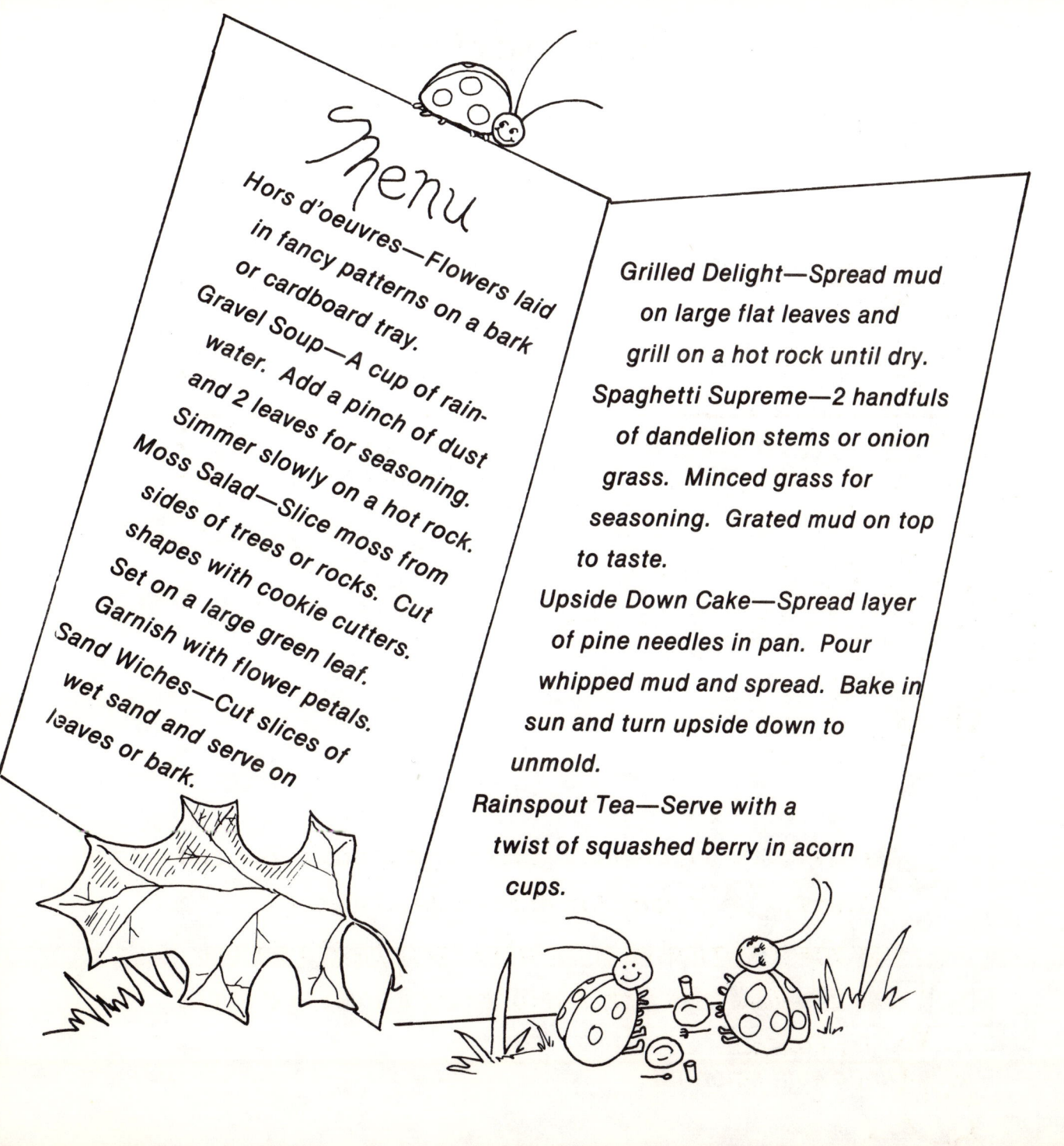

Menu

Hors d'oeuvres—Flowers laid in fancy patterns on a bark or cardboard tray.

Gravel Soup—A cup of rain-water. Add a pinch of dust and 2 leaves for seasoning. Simmer slowly on a hot rock.

Moss Salad—Slice moss from sides of trees or rocks. Cut shapes with cookie cutters. Set on a large green leaf. Garnish with flower petals.

Sand Wiches—Cut slices of wet sand and serve on leaves or bark.

Grilled Delight—Spread mud on large flat leaves and grill on a hot rock until dry.

Spaghetti Supreme—2 handfuls of dandelion stems or onion grass. Minced grass for seasoning. Grated mud on top to taste.

Upside Down Cake—Spread layer of pine needles in pan. Pour whipped mud and spread. Bake in sun and turn upside down to unmold.

Rainspout Tea—Serve with a twist of squashed berry in acorn cups.

YOU CAN BE A SCIENTIST!

You can be

. . . a backyard scientist

. . . a bathtub scientist

. . . a sidewalk scientist

. . . a windowsill scientist

FOR YOUR SCIENCE PROJECTS

Ask a grownup to help you gather these things and put them

in a big dish pan or pail so that they will be ready

when you need them.

Don't forget to put your science equipment

away neatly when a project is

finished!

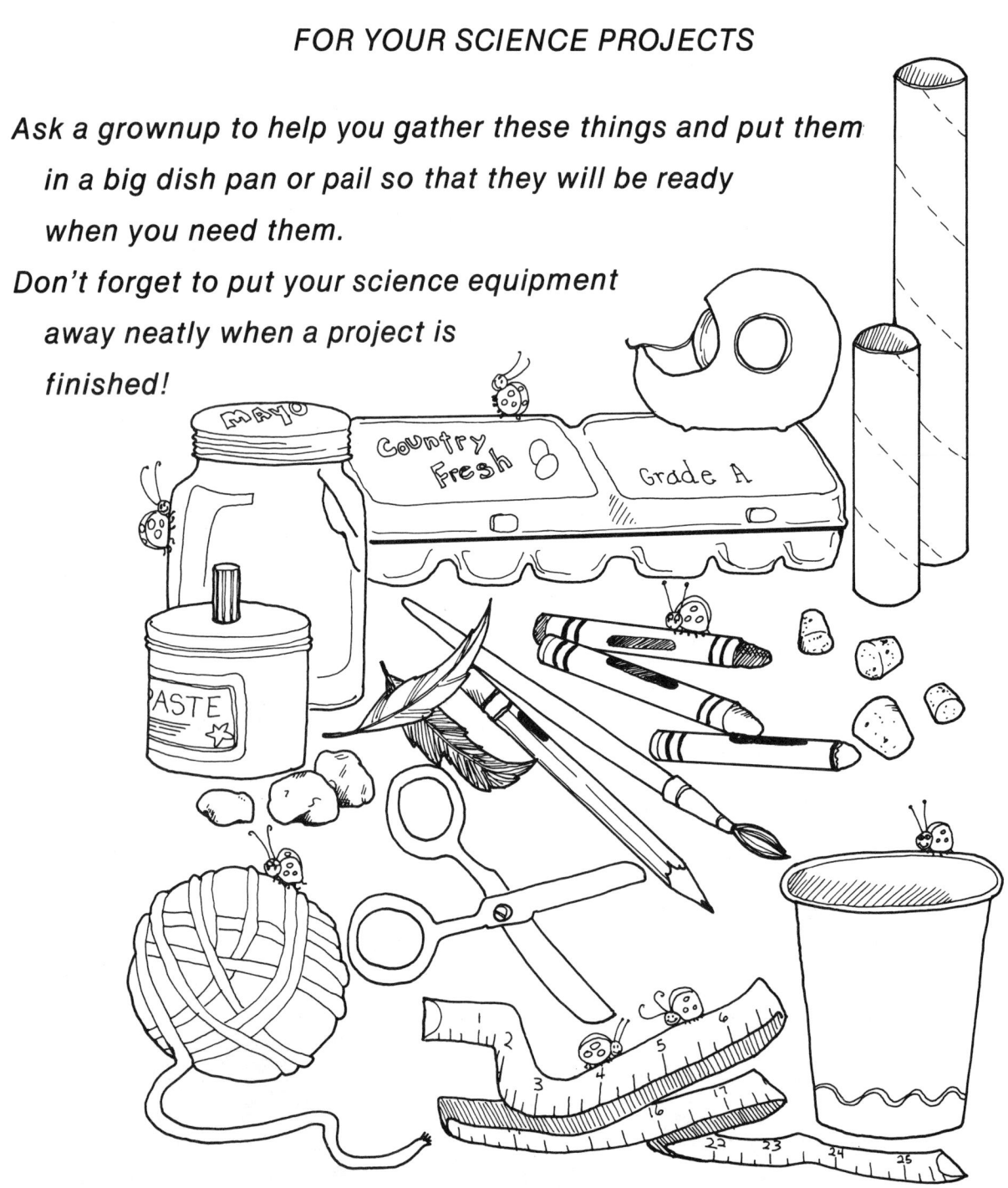

SHARPEN YOUR SENSES

Take a Listening Walk

Listen carefully to the sounds all around you. Count the animal sounds, the sounds made by machines and sounds made by the wind.

Have a Tasting Party

Collect some foods such as lemon, stick cinnamon, dill pickle, uncooked oatmeal, salt, ketchup and cocoa.

Ask a friend to close his eyes and see if he can identify the food.

Make a Feeling Box

Cut a hole big enough to put your hand through in the top of a box. Put a lot of different kinds of things to feel in the box.

You could use sand paper, velvet, cotton, spaghetti, a rock, a leaf and a mirror. Ask a friend to reach in, feel one thing at a time, describe it and try to guess what it is.

Stage a Seeing Contest

Put ten things on a table and cover them with a towel.

Take the towel off just for a minute and try to see how many of the things you can name when they are covered again.

Ask two friends to play the game and see who can name the most things.

Smell and Tell

Ask a grownup to find six unusual things in your house.

Close your eyes or wear a blindfold and smell the things one at a time.

Try to tell the names just by smelling.

There are many different sizes, shapes and colors of living things.

They all need air, water and food to live.

You are a living thing!

Describe yourself to a friend.

How long do you think you would live without air, water and food?

You need shelter, too!!

Plants are living things.
Plant several bean seeds in each
of two small containers.
Place one in a sunny spot and one
in a dark corner or
closet.
Water lightly each day.

Which one grows fastest?
Why?

LIVING THINGS GROW AND CHANGE

Match the babies with the grownups.

How many living things can you find on this page? Name them.

Can you find at least 8 non-living things that begin with the letter P?

CATCH AN INSECT IN A GLASS JAR

Screw the top on and punch some holes in it for air.

Ask a friend to join you in observing the insect.

Take turns telling each other about the insect.

Help! Don't forget to free the insect outside when you have finished.

You will want to tell each other about its size, shape, color and movement.

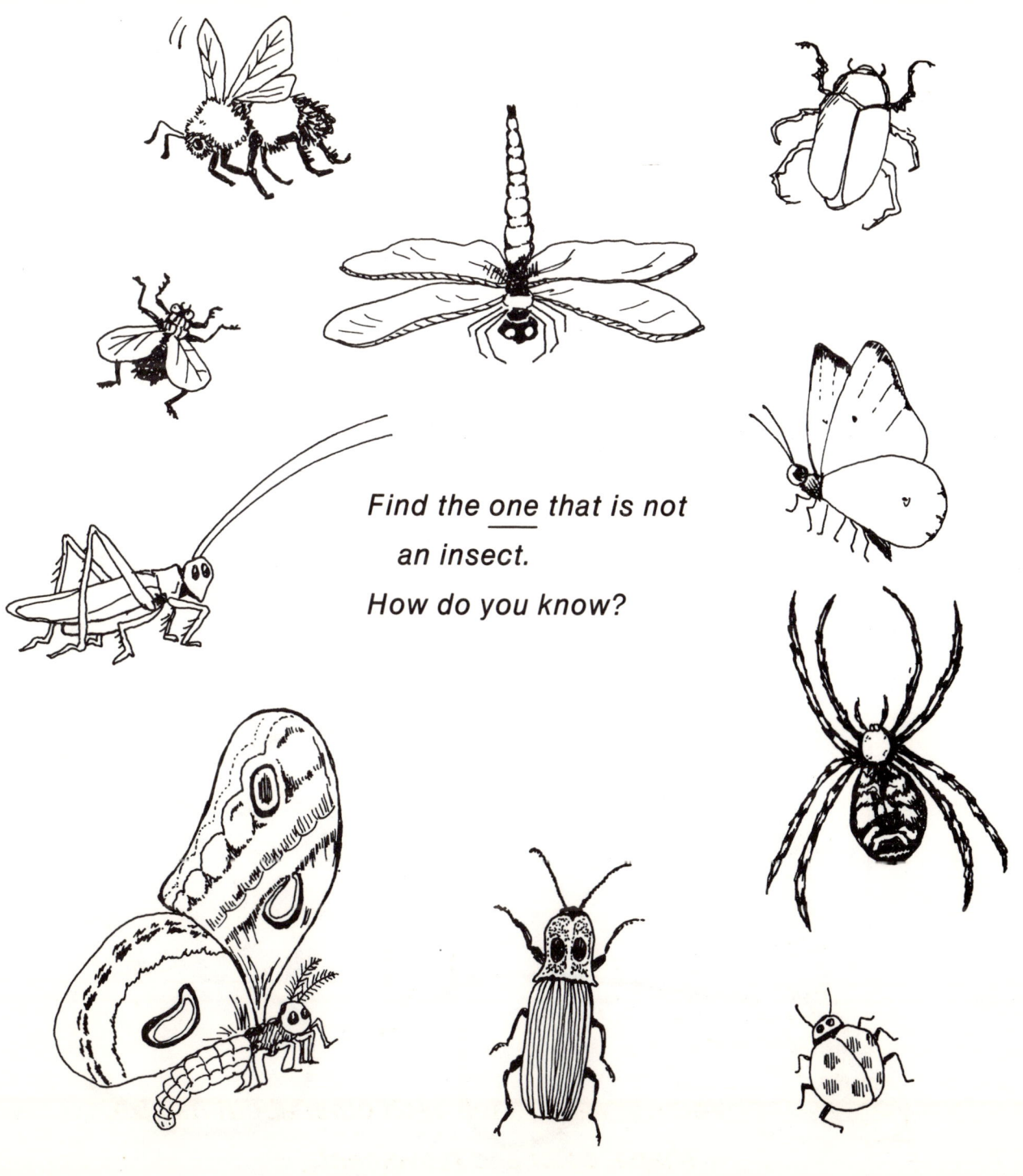

Find the <u>one</u> that is not an insect.

How do you know?

BUG-A-BOO!

Help these insects, bugs and spiders find their homes.

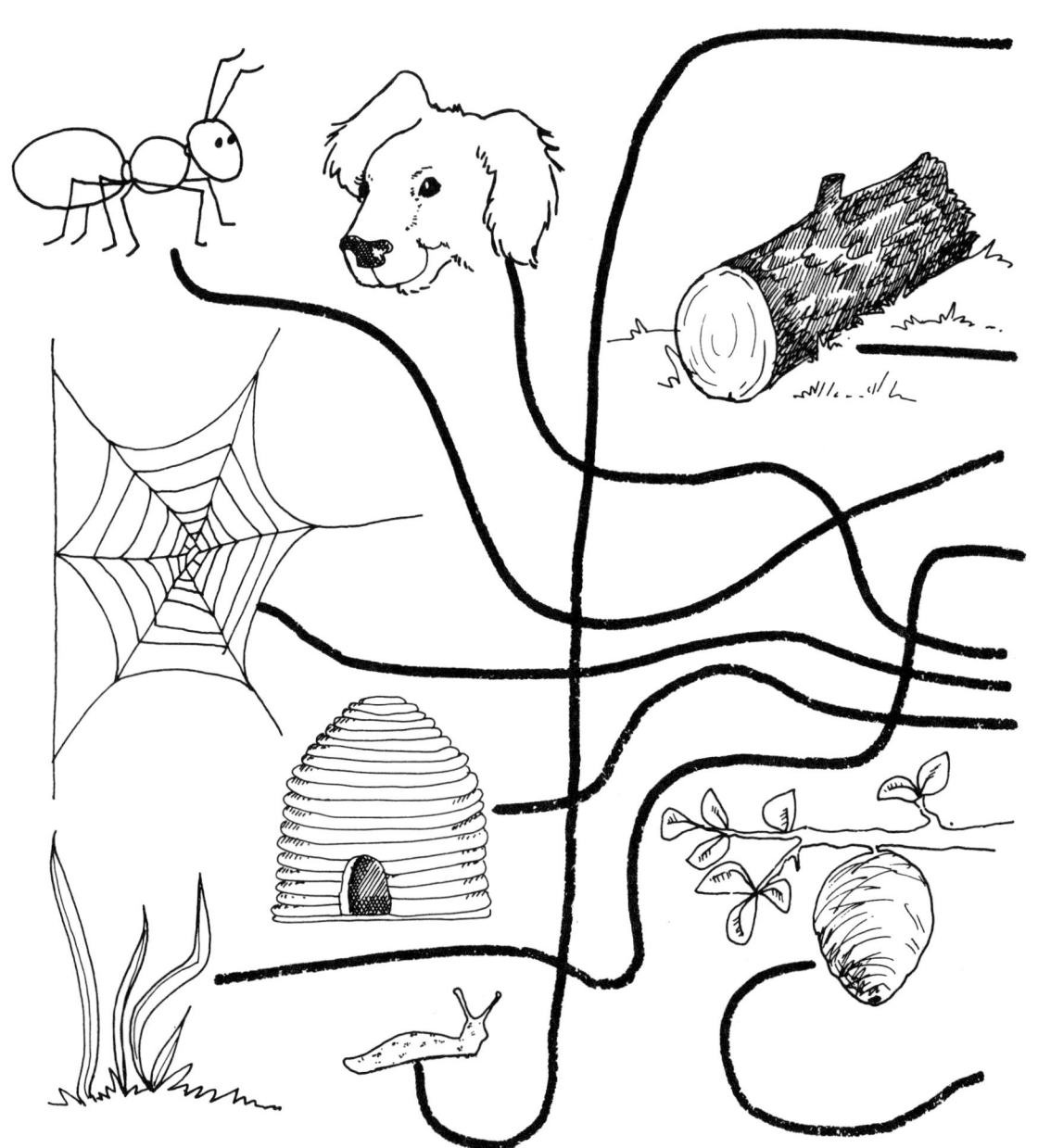

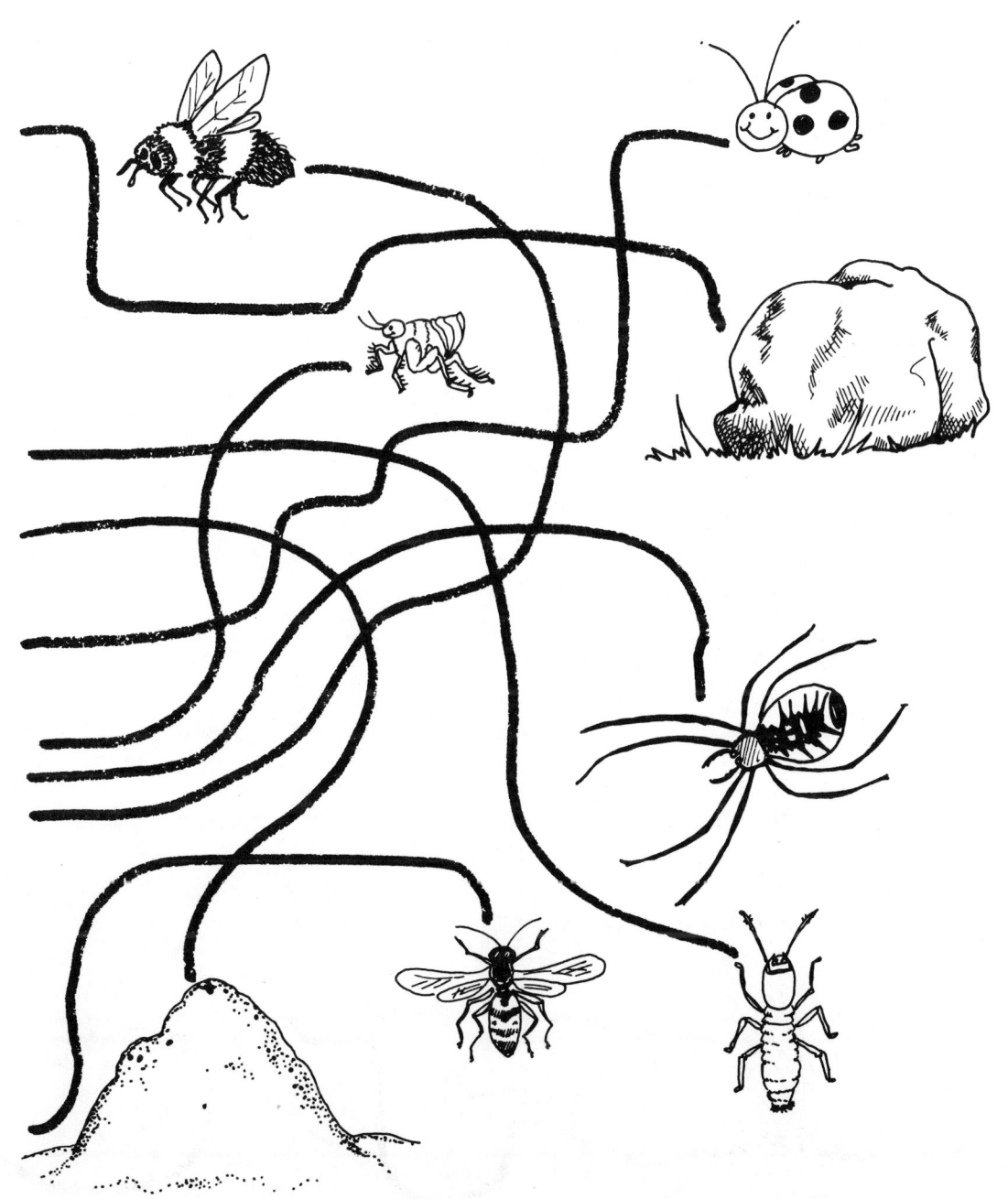

PUT A HOPTOAD IN YOUR POCKET!

Put each animal in the right pocket.

animals that walk

animals that fly

How many animals can go in two or more pockets?

animals that crawl

animals that swim

animals that hop

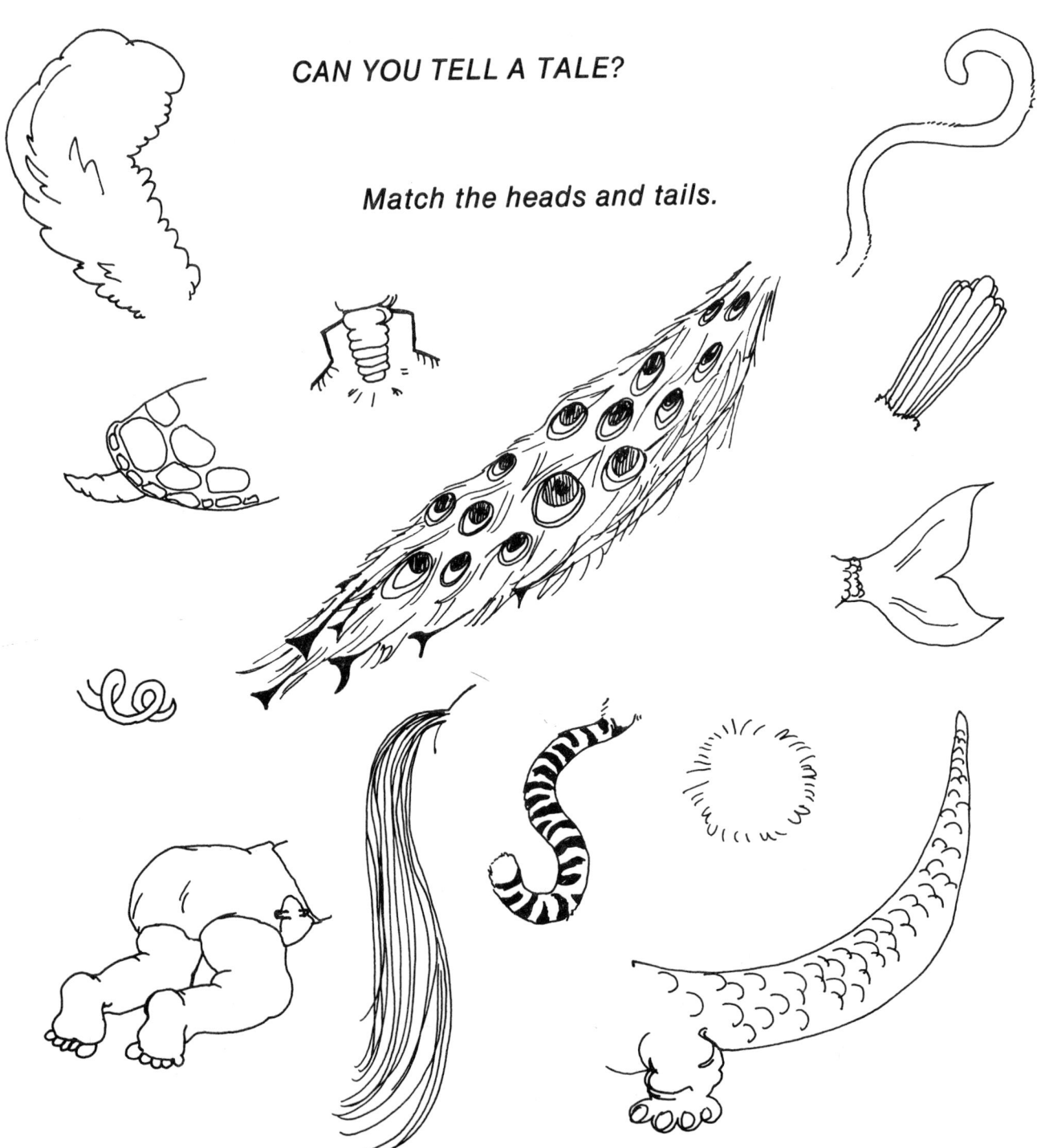

CAN YOU TELL A TALE?

Match the heads and tails.

CRITTER CAGES

Here are some ideas for making cages for critters.

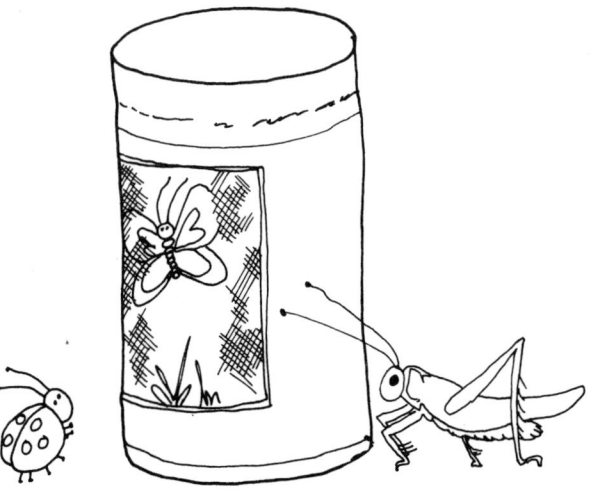

Critter cages are only
for keeping animals
to watch for a
brief time.

Don't forget to let
your critter go free after
you've watched for a while.

THE HOME OF MY ANTS . . . .

Put several inches of sand or soil in a large jar or aquarium.

Add about 6 ounces of water, some ants and some food scraps.

Add a piece of cotton.

Keep the cotton damp by adding 6 or 8 drops of water to it
   each day.

Watch your ants live and work.

   (Provide tiny food crumbs, specks of hamburger, a drop of
      honey on a crumb or a
      crumb soaked in sugar
      water for food.)

GROW A REAL LIVE MONSTER!

Put a potato in a
bag and hide it in a dark
corner for a few weeks.

Take a peek now and then to see how your
monster is growing.

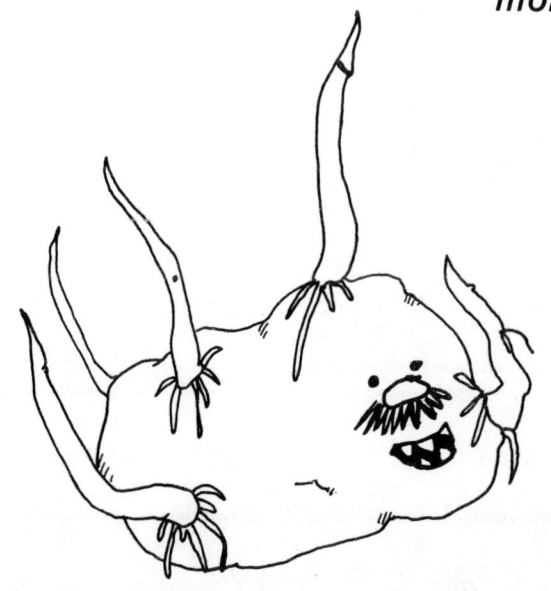

After a few weeks, let him out.
Use a magic marker to give him some
eyes and a nose.
Scare your friends with the monster!

ABOUT SEEDS

Seeds travel from one place to another in lots of interesting ways.

Ask a grownup to read the story of "Johnny Appleseed" to you.

To make a seed poster, you will need a big sheet of paper, some
paste and as many interesting seeds as you can find.
Paste the seeds on the paper and hang it on the kitchen wall.
Ask everyone in your family to name the seeds.

MAKE A V.I.P. CUBE . . .
(for a Very Important Plant!)

Use a small square box.
On the top, paste a picture of the
    plant.
On side 1, put a drawing of a place where
    the plant likes to grow.

On side 2, paste a picture that
    shows how the plant is used by
    or affects people.
On side 3, put a story about
    the plant.
On side 4, show something that
    could be made from this plant.

Did you know that . . .

SOME PLANTS MAKE GOOD FOOD!!

Bread begins with grains of wheat
And cakes from corn are made?
Berries, grapes and oranges
Are what's in jam and marmalade?
Beans are ground for coffee?
Leaves are soaked for tea?
And lots of seed make tasty treats
—Like rye and sesame?

I sure am glad there's a peanut plant!

PEANUT BUTTER

JAM

The mint and fruity flavors
Of gum and candy bars
Aren't really made on the Milky Way
By little men from Mars.
For most of the tastes you've learned to love
Were plants not long ago.
Plants' seeds and leaves and flowers
   and fruits
Make many foods we know!!

Never eat a plant you don't know! Some plants are not good to eat. Some are even poisonous!

**GROW A GARDEN
ON
YOUR WINDOWSILL**

Plant parsley seeds on a damp sponge
and you'll have parsley a'plenty!

Make a potato planter for a friend.
Cut a large potato in half, scoop out
  the middle and plant some grass or bean seed.
You could use pipe cleaners, buttons and bows to
  give your planter a special personality.

Put carrot tops in a shallow bowl
of water and wait for the green
lace to appear.

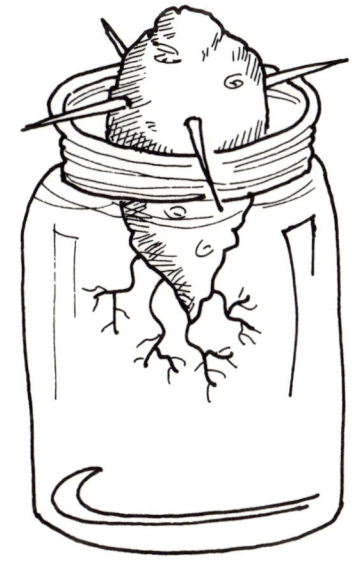

If you rest a sweet potato on tooth picks
in a jar of water, you'll soon be the
owner of a lovely trailing potato vine.

Place dry lima beans on a bed of damp
cotton on top of a glass of water and—
Presto-Change-O! It won't be
long before you see bean sprouts!

Invite some friends in to see your garden and
tell them all about how it grew.

MIX-UP, FIX-UP

What a mixed-up world!
Can you put everything back where
it belongs?

Draw the pictures here or just draw a line
from each object to where it should be.

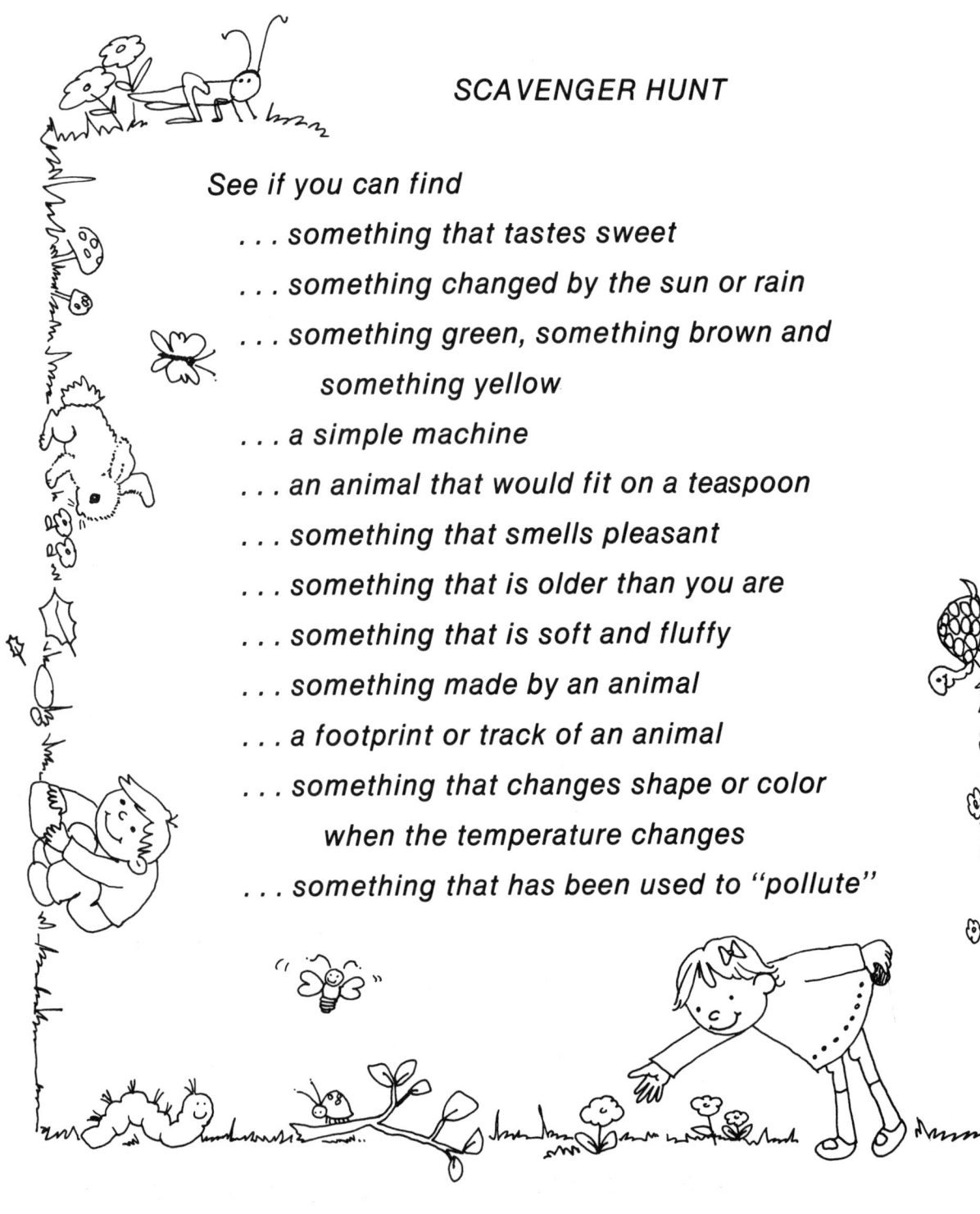

SCAVENGER HUNT

See if you can find

... something that tastes sweet

... something changed by the sun or rain

... something green, something brown and something yellow

... a simple machine

... an animal that would fit on a teaspoon

... something that smells pleasant

... something that is older than you are

... something that is soft and fluffy

... something made by an animal

... a footprint or track of an animal

... something that changes shape or color when the temperature changes

... something that has been used to "pollute"

GROW YOUR OWN SPECIAL PLACE!

Choose an outdoor place that is private.

Pound a circle of short stakes in the ground.

Ask someone taller to pound a tall stake or pole in the center of the circle.

Great idea!

Attach a string from each short stake to the pole.

Plant peas at the base of each stake.

As the plants grow, train them to wind along the string.

When they reach the pole, you will have a special private place of your own where you may hide and think.

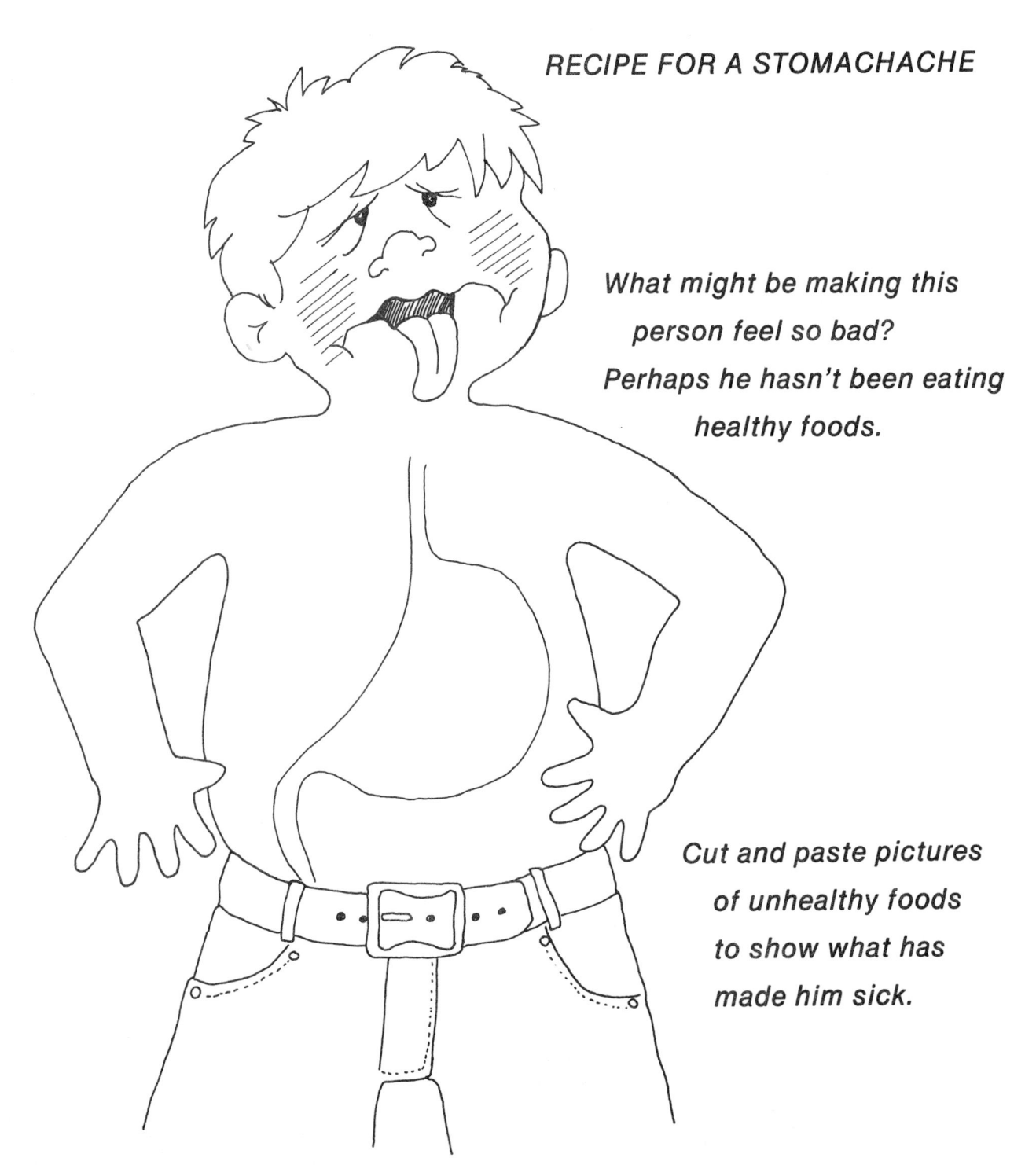

RECIPE FOR A STOMACHACHE

What might be making this person feel so bad? Perhaps he hasn't been eating healthy foods.

Cut and paste pictures of unhealthy foods to show what has made him sick.

Cut and paste pictures to set this table with lots of healthy things to eat.

WANT TO MAKE SOME WAVES?

Find a pickle jar or a jelly jar with a good, tight-fitting screw top.

Fill the jar a little less than half full of white vinegar.

Finish filling the jar almost to the top with cooking oil.

Screw on the top and gently roll the jar back
and forth to cause tiny, ocean-like waves.

Add a paper raft or boat, if you like.

What do you think causes the waves?

Maybe you can make up an ocean song to sing while
you are watching the waves.

WHAT DOES YOUR SALT GARDEN GROW?

Salt . . . of course!

Find some porous stones or pieces of coal.

Fill a cereal bowl about half full of water.

Keep adding salt and stirring until no more salt will dissolve
   in the water.

Then stir in a tablespoon of vinegar.

Now fill the bowl of
salty water with
the stones you
   have collected.

In one day, the
salt crystals
will begin to
"grow" and your
bowl of stones
will begin to
look like a
"magic" castle!

AN EXPERIMENT WITH AIR

Set up two big, heavy books.

Puff up your cheeks and try to blow them down.

Can you?

Now set the books close together.

Blow up a balloon between the books.

Oh-oh—look what happens!

So—you really can blow a heavy book

down with air!

TIME CHANGES THINGS

Can you tell about the changes you see here?

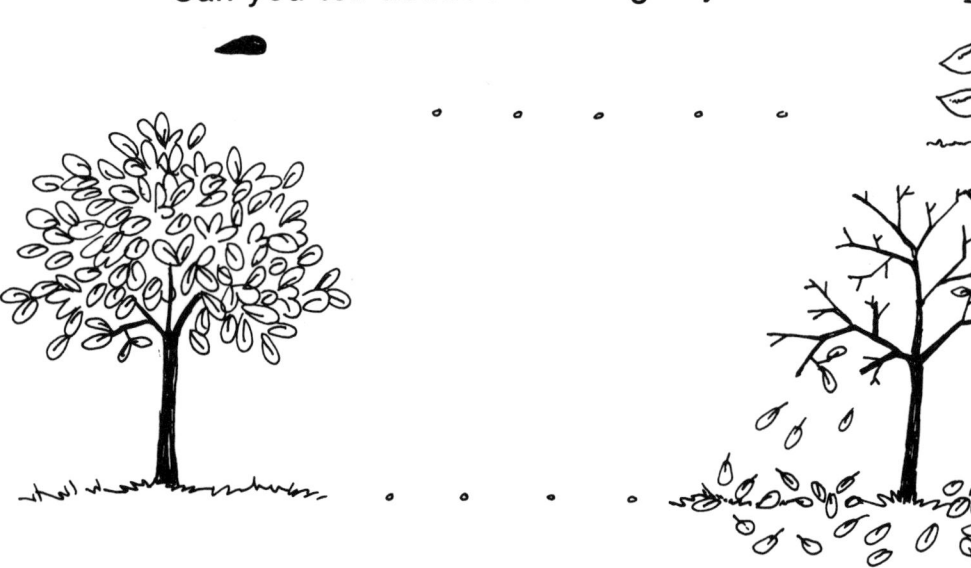

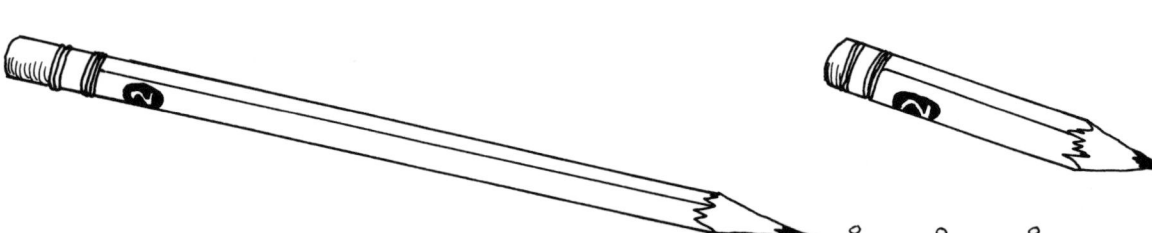

Which of these things will time change
most quickly?

Which will change slowly?

WHICH MACHINE

. . . would you use to cool a hot room??

. . . would you use to heat a room on a cold night?

Which three would you use to clean the house?

Can you find three carpenter's tools?

Which two would you use in the yard?

Which machine would you use just for fun?

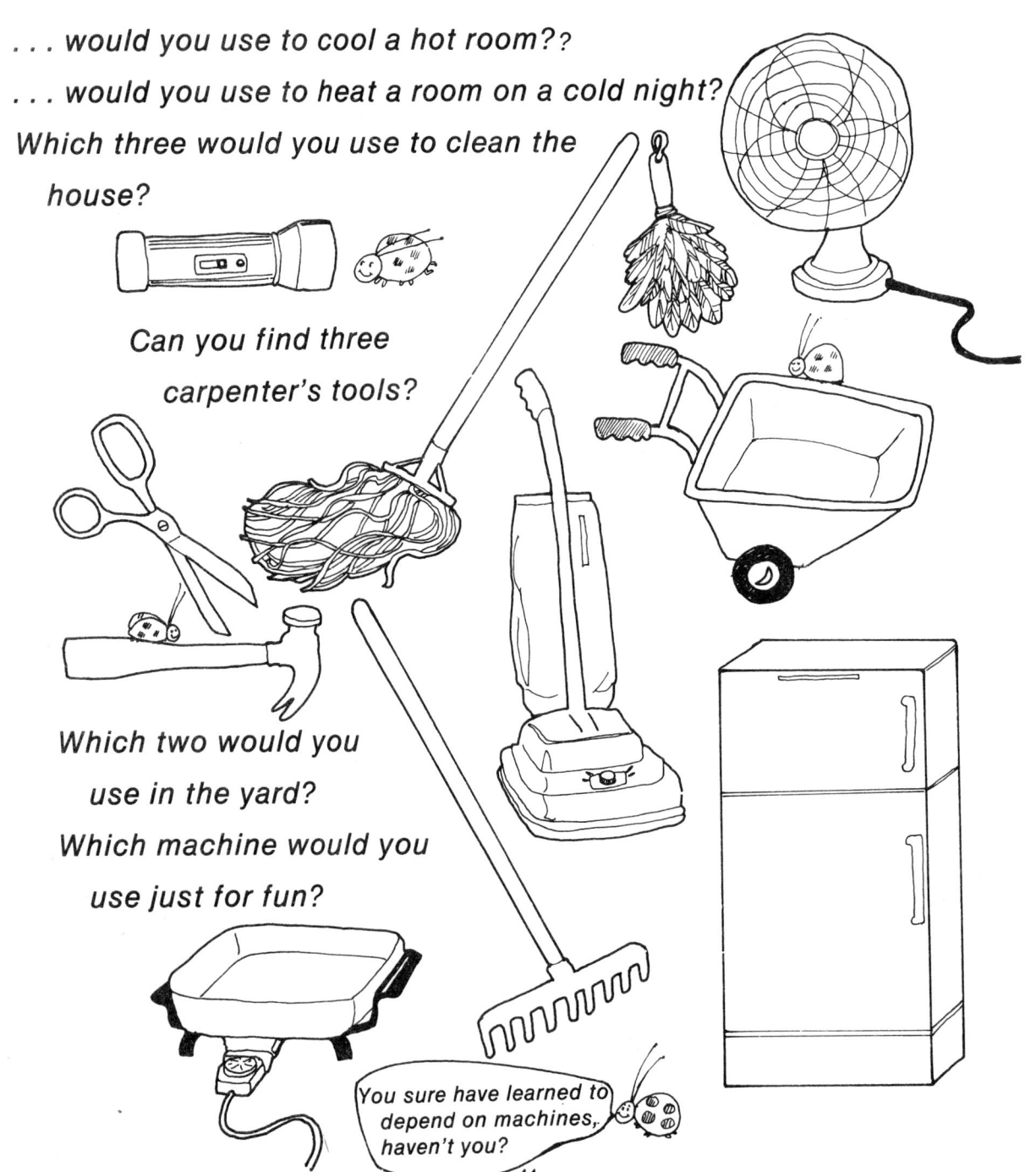

You sure have learned to depend on machines, haven't you?

Look all around your house to find the machines
used to make work easier.

How many can you find in the kitchen?

Don't forget to look in the bathroom and in
the bedroom.

Try to find one electric machine, one wheeled one and one battery-
operated one.

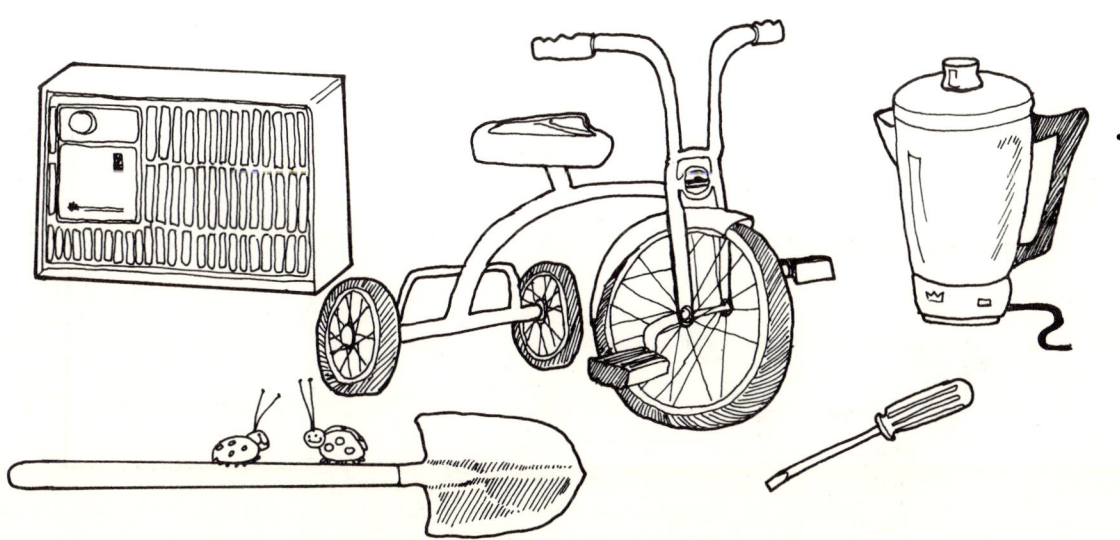

EXPERIMENTS WITH ICE

Which is the fastest way to melt
  an ice cube?
Experiment to see!

Hold it in your hand.
Place it in the sun.
Place it on a light-colored surface.
Place it on a dark-colored
  surface.

Can you think of other ways?

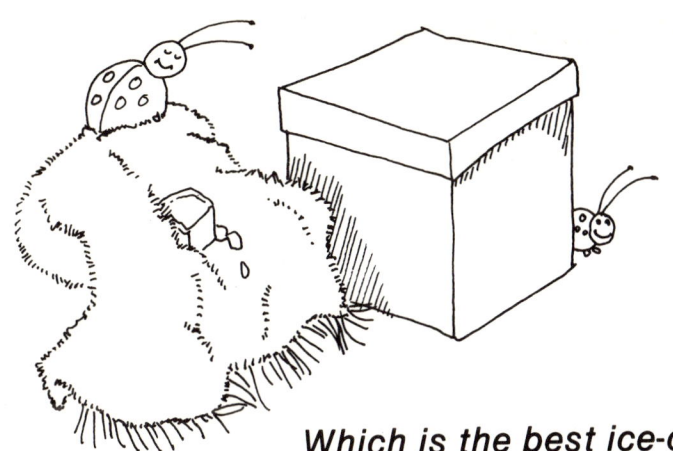

Which is the best ice-cube keeper?

A cloth or towel

A cardboard box

An egg carton

A pile of sand

A pile of sawdust

Experiment to see!

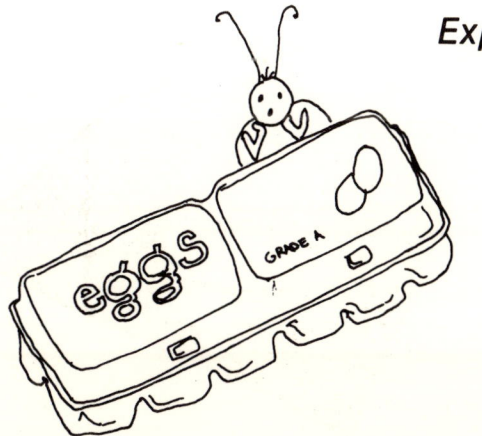

NICE ICE SHAPES

Use a variety of containers to fill with water and freeze:

shallow round pans (to make pancake shapes)

cylinders and thin tubes (to make tall shapes)

balloons (to make round

shapes)

cake or jello molds (to make donut shapes)

squares

Experiment to see: Which shapes melt the fastest?

How does each shape float?

LOTS OF FUN WITH GUESS-BOXES

This is a game you can play with your friends.
Find 5 or 6 objects in your house that may be
identified by using one or more of
the senses.

Put each in a box and
wrap it like a present.
Make a tiny picture of what is
in each box and tape it on
the bottom.
Ask your friends to try to guess
what is in each box by using
all their senses.

They can feel the box, smell the box

shake the box and listen to the contents move.

When they have made a guess,
let them look at the
picture taped to the bottom
to check their guesses.
Then they may open the box
to see.

GO TRAILBLAZING!

Make an outdoor trail for someone to follow.

You can do this by leaving markers at short distances along the way.

(Be careful not to damage the environment, and remember to clean up any mess you make!)

TRY THESE TRICKY QUESTIONS!

Ask someone smart to help you find answers to these questions.

Watch out! The pictures will trick you!

What causes lightning?

Ah... Ah...
Ah....

What causes allergies?

choo

Where does a baby come from?

How do wild geese find their way south every winter?

Why would a jacket left outside on a night when there was no rain be damp the next morning?

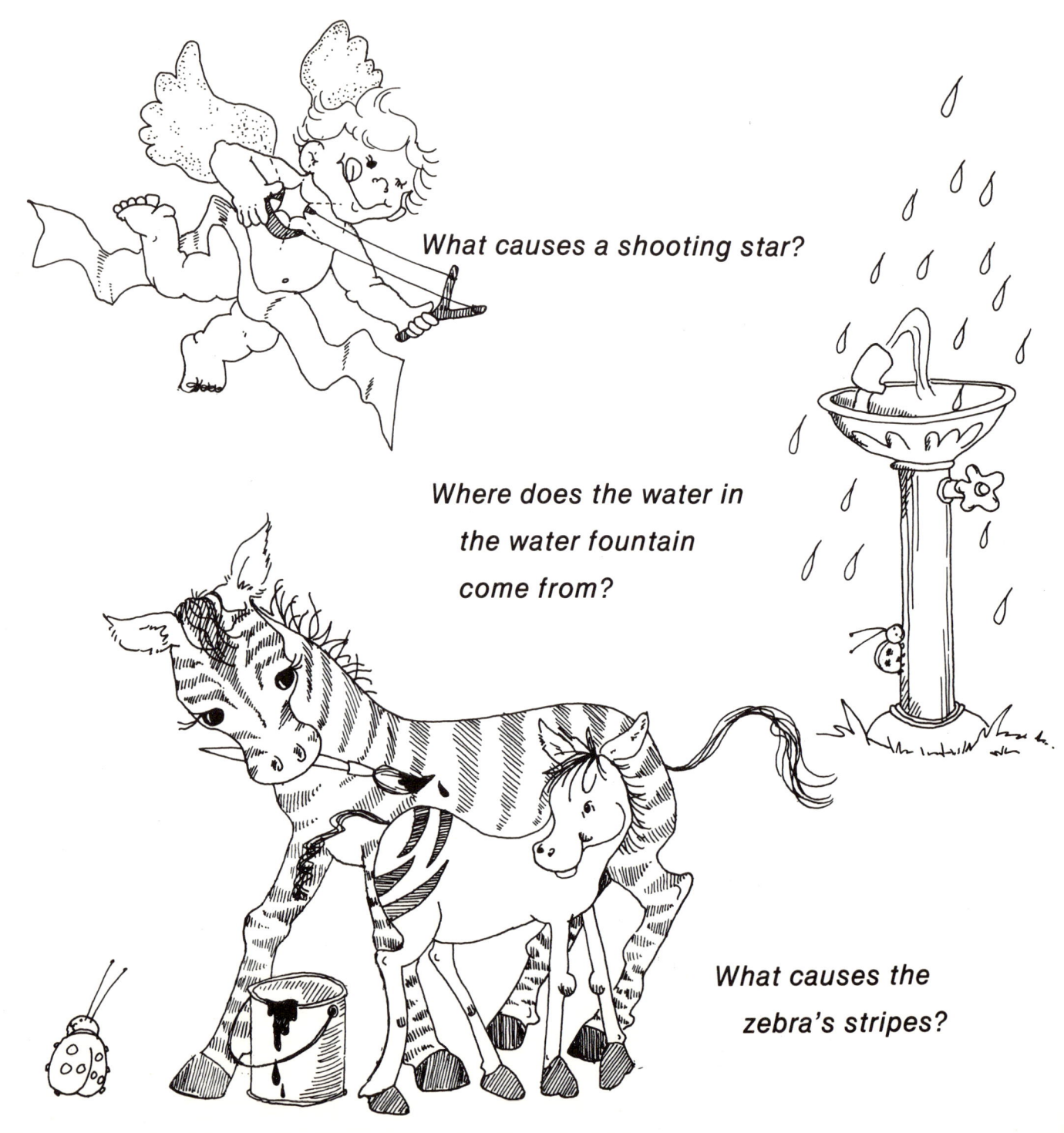

What causes a shooting star?

Where does the water in
the water fountain
come from?

What causes the
zebra's stripes?

How does a rainbow get its colors?

How many years does it take for a giant oak tree to grow from a tiny acorn?

You didn't let those tricky pictures fool you, did you?

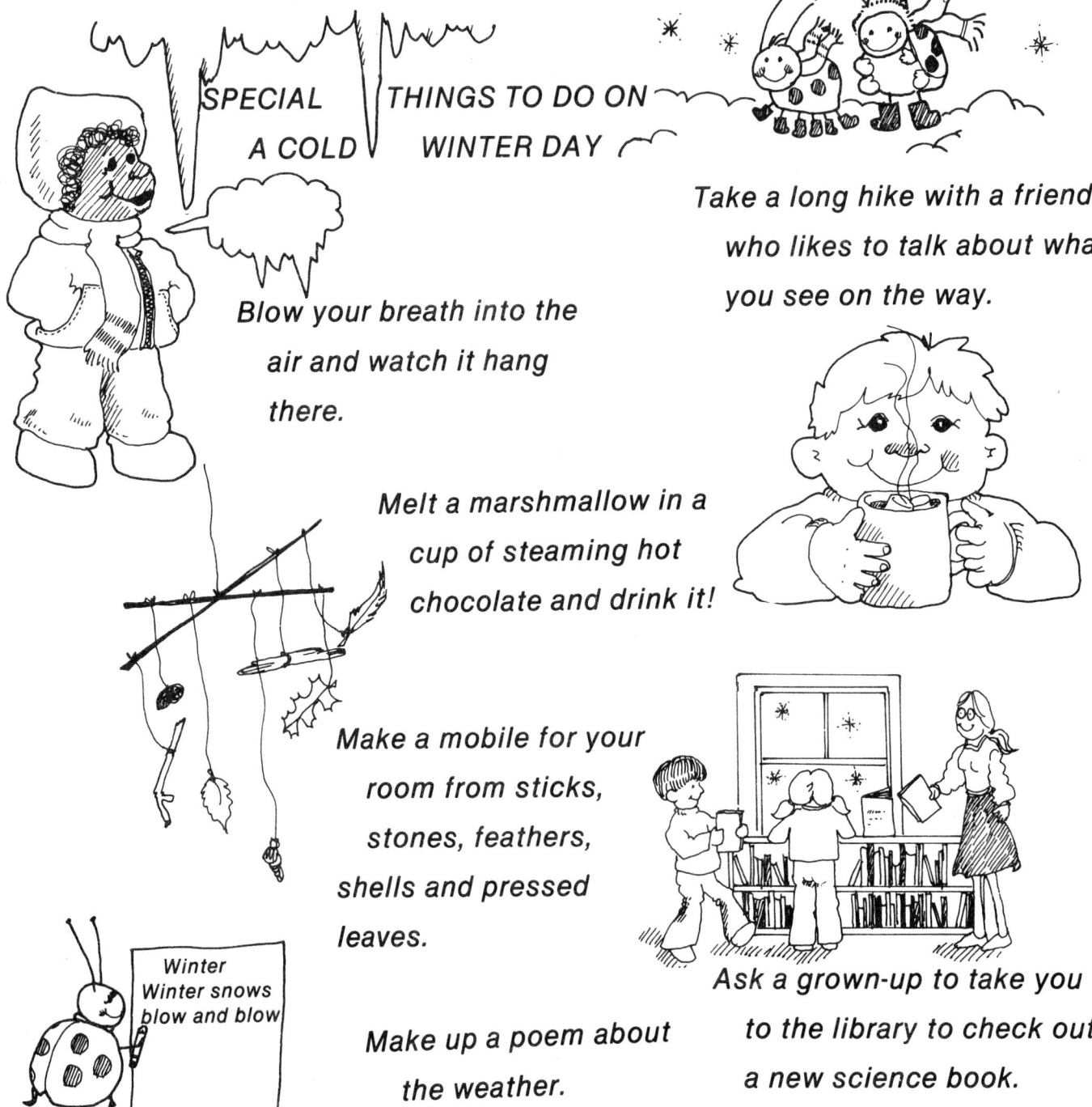

SPECIAL THINGS TO DO ON A COLD WINTER DAY

Blow your breath into the air and watch it hang there.

Take a long hike with a friend who likes to talk about what you see on the way.

Melt a marshmallow in a cup of steaming hot chocolate and drink it!

Make a mobile for your room from sticks, stones, feathers, shells and pressed leaves.

Winter
Winter snows
blow and blow

Make up a poem about the weather.

Ask a grown-up to take you to the library to check out a new science book.

LOVELY THINGS TO DO ON A WARM SUMMER DAY

Make a daisy chain for someone you love.

Fly a kite.

Make ice cold lemonade for your whole family.

Blow some soap bubbles through a straw.

Try to find a butterfly to watch for a while.

Love a ladybug!